P9-DHF-470

Emmy
the Exaggerating
Elephant

Fenton
the Fearful Frog

Gertie
the Grungy Goat

the Happy
Hamster

the Impatient
Iguana

Ollie
the Obedient
Ostrich

Perry
the Polite
Porcupine

Queenie
the Quiet Quail

Rupert
the Resourceful
Rhinoceros

Ziggy
the Zippy Zebra

Wendy
the Wise
Woodchuck

Xavier
the X-ploring
Xenops

Yori
the Yucky Yak

The next morning when Perry woke up, the sun was shining brightly.

"What a perfect day to sit by the pool and read!" he exclaimed.

So after Perry ate his pancakes, he took his book and settled himself in a comfortable chair near the pool.

Perry smiled to himself as he started to read his book.

Always say PLEASE *when you want something and* THANK YOU *when you get it.*

"Yes, I learned that a long time ago," Perry said. He read on.

Always say HELLO *when you arrive and* GOOD–BYE *when you leave.*

SHAKE HANDS *and* SMILE *when you meet someone.*

DON'T INTERRUPT *when someone is speaking.*

SAY EXCUSE ME *if you bump into someone or if you make a mistake.*

Perry knew all those manners already.

Perry was happily turning the pages of his book when he heard the doorbell ring.

"Perry! Perry! Is anybody home?" said a voice at the front door.

"I'm not expecting anyone," Perry said to himself. He put down his book and went to see what all the noise was about.

Perry opened the door. Tina the Truthful Tiger and Connie the Cuddly Cat were there.

"Hello, Perry," said Tina. "It's such a warm day, Connie and I thought we'd drop by for a swim in your pool. I hope you don't mind."

Perry knew it was polite to make his friends feel welcome but inside he was thinking, "Will I ever be able to read my book?" He smiled. "Well...er...Come right in," he said.

"Thank you!" whooped Tina and Connie. They followed Perry through the house to the backyard. Then they jumped in the pool with a *splash!*

Tina and Connie weren't the only ones who dropped
by for a swim. Soon Bradley the Brave Bear arrived, and
so did Monty the Mimicking Mouse and Albert the
Absent-minded Alligator.

"Hi, Perry," said Bradley. "Perfect day, isn't it?"

"Hi, Perry," said Monty. "Perfect day, isn't it?"

"Yes, I guess it was...er...*is* a perfect day," Perry said, a little sadly. "It sure is hard being polite sometimes," he thought to himself.

Perry watched his friends having a wonderful time splashing in the pool. Then he had an idea! He took his book and quietly slipped into the house.

Perry ran to his bedroom, and found the perfect hiding place: his closet. He pushed his shoes aside, sat down on the floor, opened his book and continued to read.

ALWAYS BE PUNCTUAL. *Do not keep people waiting.*

Be respectful of others, but RESPECT YOURSELF, *too.*

"That's a *new* one. I wonder what it means," Perry said. He read on.

If you really don't want to do something, YOU CAN SAY "NO" POLITELY.

Perry's eyes lit up! "Oh, my goodness!" he said. "I never thought of it that way before! Being polite means treating people kindly—but it doesn't mean that I have to say yes *all* the time. I can say no in a kindly way, too!"

Perry ran out to the pool. "Listen, everybody!" he called. The AlphaPets stopped playing and listened to him.

"I want you all to have a good time, and I don't want to hurt your feelings, but ... but ..." Perry couldn't continue.

"What's wrong?" Connie asked.

"Please tell us!" said Tina.

"Well," Perry said. "You are all my friends and I love you, but I didn't expect you to drop in on me. I'm sorry, but I have other plans today."

"There! I said it," thought Perry. His heart was pounding.

The AlphaPets gathered around their friend.

"I hope you're not upset," Perry said softly.

"Not at all," said Bradley. "You were as polite as always. And it was brave of you to remind us to be considerate of you, too."

"Don't forget," said Albert, "friends should always tell each other how they really feel."

"Well, we'd better get going," said Tina. "Thank you for a very nice time, Perry. And next time, we'll remember to call first. Right?"

"Right!" everyone shouted.

"Right!" said Monty.

Will you please read these words with me?
Thank you.

purse

pencil

pineapple

pie

pajama

puzzle

pillow

pickle

Look back in this book and try to find these and other things that begin with P.

Know Your Alphabet

Aa Bb

Gg Hh

Mm Nn Oo Pp

Uu Vv Ww